ANTHONY WILEY

SEARCH FOR A SONG

Illustrations: Per Illum

Anthony Wiley: Search for a Song
Teen Readers, Level 3

Series editor: Ulla Malmmose

© 1998 by Anthony Wiley and
Aschehoug Dansk Forlag A/S
Copenhagen
ISBN Denmark 87-11-09079-0

Printed in Denmark by
Sangill Grafisk Produktion
Holme Olstrup

The Band

Rocky played a guitar chord that shook the walls of the garage and ended the song. He looked around at the other four members of the band and they seemed to be happy about how the song had sounded. Before they could talk, the door to the garage opened and Roger Capelli's father came in.

"OK kids, it's a little bit late and a little bit loud, so why don't you call it a night. We don't want Mr. Willis calling up and complaining again," Roger's father said.

"One more ... " Roger started to say, but his father pointed at his watch.

"It's almost nine o'clock and you kids have to go to school tomorrow. You can practice again after school," his father said, and walked out.

"Hey Egghead, I thought you said your father liked our music," Peter "Goes" Dodge called to him. All the kids called Peter "Goes", because when he told a story, he would say something like, 'and then he goes ...and when she heard it, she goes'. He always used the word goes instead of using the correct word, said. No matter how many times his teachers or parents corrected him, he always said it.

"He does like it," Egghead answered. "But it is getting late." Roger's head did not look like an egg at all, but since he was so good in school and because he loved computers and electronic musical instruments, all the kids called him Egghead – in the same way many other smart youngsters are called eggheads. He started to move some of the *synthesizers* that formed a circle

---

synthesizer, electronic musical instrument, like a piano

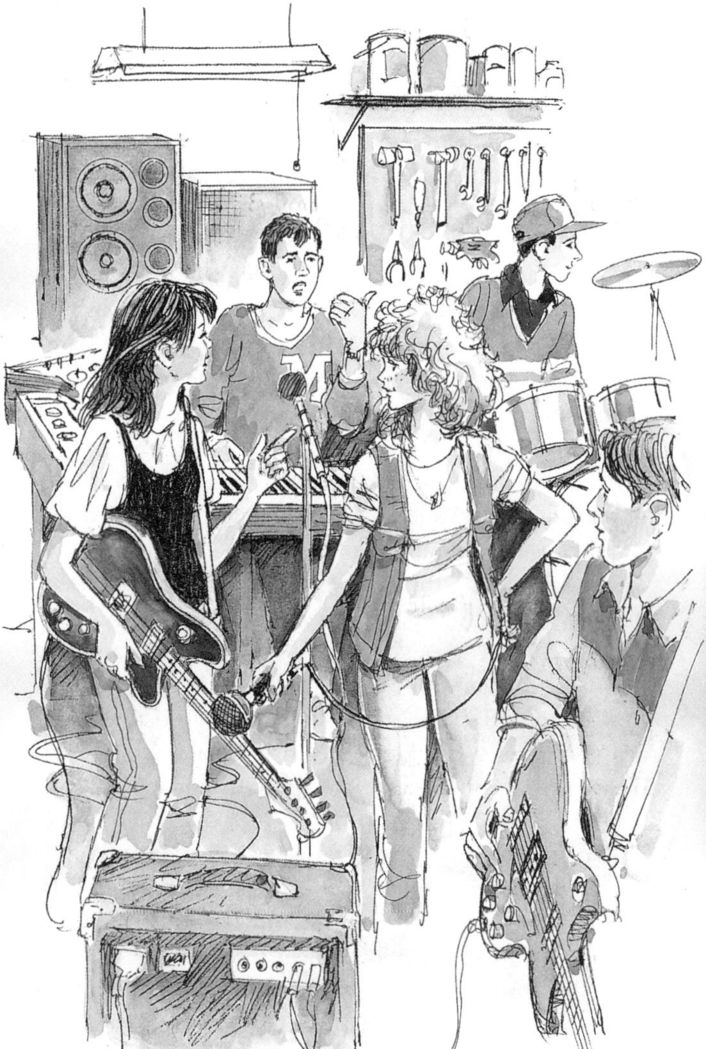

around him. "And I don't want Mr. Willis complaining. He said he would call the police the next time he heard us playing after nine. Last month he put a little tape recorder outside his door. He brought the tape over so my father could listen to how much noise we made. You could hardly hear the music, but my father says we have to turn down the sound and not play after nine," Egghead said. Mr. Willis was the closest neighbor, even though his house was almost a five-minute walk down the country road.

"Let's put our equipment away and we can figure out a name for the band," Bob "Rocky" Stone said, and put his guitar into its case.

"Good idea," Jenny Zbinski, the bass player, said. "My fingers hurt. I don't think I could play another note."

The band had been practicing since just after school let out at three. They took one break to gobble down pizzas and then it was back to work. The five of them wanted to finish the sounds for what they hoped would be their first single. All of them loved music, and dreamed that one day they would be stars. They used the Capellis' garage to practice. Egghead's father worked in a store that sold stereos, computers televisions and other electronic products. He would often take broken equipment home - things that customers no longer wanted - and he or Egghead would fix them. In this way, they had built a sound studio in the garage.

"Hey Z," Goes called to Jenny. "Could you help me with my drums?"

"Give me a dollar," Z answered.

"I'll give you a kiss instead," Goes replied, even though in all of his 16 years of life, he had never kissed a girl and wasn't sure he wanted to start with Z – she was one of the boys, just as the singer and keyboard player Shelly Rodman was.

Z rolled her eyes and said, "I'll tell you what. You keep the kiss and I'll give you the dollar instead." She walked over to help him.

Once they had cleared up the garage, they sat around the little table in the corner and talked about a name for the band. After a few minutes they realized they would probably never agree on a name.

"I want a cool name for me on the album," Rocky said. "You know, something like Beck, or Flea, or Edge, just like the stars."

"And I want my name to be Sleeve. That's cool!" Goes said.

"Why, because you always wipe your nose on your sleeve?" Shelly asked, and the others laughed. Goes grabbed a piece of pizza crust that was on the table and threw it at her. It bounced off the top of her head.

Before an all-out battle could start, Jenny said, "I want to be called Ruby."

"Ruby!?" the others repeated, looking at her as if the loud music had made her lose her mind.

"Wait a minute! Wait a minute!" Egghead shouted. The others looked at him. "I want to be Egghead. My mother hates it when you guys call me that, but I like it. Anyway, we all have names, Goes is Goes, Rocky is Rocky, Z is Z and ..." They all looked at Shelly.

"I like Shelly," she said. "I don't want to give myself some name, and you guys shouldn't either. Egghead is right. Let's use the names we have."

"And before we start giving ourselves names, and thinking about the Grammy awards we'll win and all our fans," Egghead said. "I think we should make a CD first."

"Why don't you turn this place into a recording studio, Egghead?" Z asked.

"That costs a lot of money, a real lot of money. Maybe someday," he answered. "But for now, we'll have to use this." He held up his little micro-disc recorder.

The others nodded. They were all excited about what was going to happen on Saturday. Rocky had seen an advertisement in a music magazine a few weeks earlier. The advertisement had been placed by a music scout who was looking for new talent. The five of them had practiced for a long time, and had finally made a recording of a song on Egghead's little micro-disc player. It wasn't much, but it did the job. They had sent the disc to the address in the advertisement and a woman named Sabrina Farley had telephoned Rocky. Farley said that she "loved" their sound and was sure she could make a recording of them that would make them stars. On Saturday, Farley would drive her mobile recording truck up from New York City to Trenton in the middle of New York State and cut a record. The five of them couldn't wait.

"I guess it doesn't matter that we don't have a name for the band yet," Z said. "We have to take one step at a time."

"Yeah, and right now I'm taking one step toward home. I'm dog tired," Goes said, and yawned.

"Cover your mouth when you yawn," Shelly snapped at him.

"It helps my voice. Otherwise I wouldn't be able to share the microphone with you," he said. She just looked at him as if he was a worm.

The band members said good-night to each other, and headed home. That night and the next two nights none of them were able to sleep well. They would lie in bed until it was nearly light, dreaming about their first record.

Waiting

Thursday and Friday were two very long days. Each class in school seemed to last for years, and when the five of them got together to play after school they had trouble keeping their minds on the music. Friday night lasted forever. Sabrina Farley would meet them at Egghead's house at one in the afternoon, so they had agreed they would get together at noon to have enough time to get their instruments set up.

Egghead was out of bed at seven. He jumped into his clothes and raced into the kitchen. On his way through the kitchen, he swallowed a glass of milk and ran into the garage with one slice of bread hanging out of his mouth and another in his hand. He ate while he began to set up the studio in the garage. Once he got into his world of electronics, time flew by.

At around 10:30 he heard a car door close. When he looked out the window, he saw Shelly's mother driving away and Shelly walking toward the garage.

"I couldn't wait until noon," she said as she walked into the garage. "I want to sing a little bit so my voice will be ready when Sabrina Farley gets here." Egghead continued to test the equipment while Shelly sang in the other end of the garage.

Z and Goes arrived together at around 11:45. A few minutes later, Rocky walked into the garage. His clothes were spattered with mud. Shelly looked at him and said: "Did you have to ride your mountain bike today? We have to look good for Sabrina Farley. What's she going to think when she sees you?"

"My parents are down in Utica shopping. How else could I get here?" Rocky answered. "And anyway, I wanted to see if I could make it up and over Buck Hill in less than an hour."

Shelly just shook her head.

"Hey, if you don't like the way I look, then you can look the other way," Rocky said.

"Can't you two take it easy?" Goes called to them from behind his drum set.

"Yeah, take it easy," Z added. "We're all excited about today, but there's no reason to get angry with each other."

"Why don't we go outside and wait for her," Egghead said.

Four of them went out and sat on the steps in front of Egghead's house. Goes had to finish putting his drums together, and he joined them a few minutes later.

The sun was warming the day quickly, in fact, it felt like a summer day even though it was still May. They sat silently for a while, each of them dreaming of becoming a rock star. The heavy logs of Egghead's log house *creaked* as the sun warmed them, and in the field across the road several cows chewed on grass. A few other cows were down by the little river that ran beside the house. The other kids lived in Trenton, but Egghead lived outside the village. There were no other houses close to Egghead's. It was the perfect place for the band to play their music loud without bothering anybody – anybody but Egghead's parents and younger sister, that is. And Mr. Willis.

They waited and watched all the cars zipping past on the highway, Route 12, off in the distance. Egghead's house was a short drive from the main road. Every time

---

creak, the sound made when wood bends - a floor some times creaks

11

they heard a car turning off the highway and onto Lowell Road where Egghead lived, they jumped up to see if it was a truck that could be a mobile recording studio. But each time it turned out to be one of the neighbors who lived along Lowell Road, or Alfred Drive that went up in the opposite direction.

"It takes around five hours to drive here from New York City," Goes said, finally breaking the silence.

"Are you sure you told her Trenton, New York? There is a Trenton in New Jersey, too," Egghead said.

"I know there's a Trenton, New Jersey. That's where George Washington crossed the Delaware, you knucklehead," Rocky said.

"That's Egghead, not knucklehead, you rock-head," Egghead replied.

Rocky jumped to his feet, but Shelly stepped between him and Egghead to stop what looked like the start of a fight. "Cut it out, you two," she ordered. "She'll get here. She probably got lost, that's all."

"Yeah. After all, Trenton looks like a tiny spot of black pepper on the map, and there are a lot of little country roads where it's easy to get lost," Goes added.

Rocky and Egghead stared at each other for a few seconds. Egghead turned to say something to Shelly and Rocky walked over to the river. He began throwing stones into the water to keep from thinking about all the waiting.

While the others argued, Z sat on the steps writing in her notebook. She would write a few lines, then scribble them out and write more.

"How's it going, Z?" Goes asked.

"Not bad," she answered. "Two or three more songs and I think we'll have enough for an album. You can take a look at this in a little while."

Z and Goes were the songwriters in the band. Z would write down lines and ideas for a song, and then Goes would re-work them. After that, they would work on the *lyrics* together. Once the lyrics were written, Egghead would take them and write the music. The five of them would then work together to find the right sound. It often took them weeks before they were satisfied with a song.

At around three o'clock, Egghead went inside the house to call Sabrina Farley. The number was for a mobile phone. When he returned they all looked up to hear what he had to say.

"I got her answering machine. It only said that she was not available at the moment, so I left a message for her to call back. She's probably got the *cell-phone* with her and will check to see if she has any messages," Egghead said.

"But she should have been here two hours ago," Z complained.

"She'll get here," Rocky said. "Don't worry." But he was beginning to worry.

A little more than a half hour later, the phone rang. Egghead ran into the house to answer it. He came out again when he saw his sister talking to one of her friends. The five of them felt their hearts sinking deeper and deeper.

"Something's wrong," Goes said, looking at his watch and seeing it was after five.

Egghead went in to call once again. Sabrina Farley's

---

lyrics, the words to a song
cell-phone, short for cellular telephone – mobile phone

answering machine said the same thing it had said before. Before he could return to his friends, his mother said: "Roger, you have to get ready. We have to be at Grandma's house in less than an hour."

Egghead told his friends about the phone call, and told them that he had to leave soon.

"Can I use your phone, Egghead? My father said he would pick me up," Shelly asked.

"Sure," he answered.

"Can I ride with you?" Z asked her.

"Me too?" Goes asked.

Shelly nodded.

Rocky said that he would wait for a while longer. He watched as Shelly, Z and Goes drove off a while later, and said good-bye to Egghead and his family when they left.

The sun was getting low, when Rocky finally got onto his bike to head for home.

Finding Sabrina

On Sunday morning, Egghead called Rocky. "She never showed up?" Egghead repeated what Rocky told him.

"No. I waited until nearly eight thirty and then I had to go home," Rocky answered. "What are we going to do now?"

"Maybe she will come today. Maybe she got lost," Egghead suggested.

Rocky did not answer, and Egghead realized that Sabrina Farley was not going to come.

"I'll try to call her number," Egghead said.

"I tried just a little while ago," Rocky said. "It was her answering machine again, so I left a message for her."

"Have you talked to the others?"

"I talked to Z last night, and she said she would tell Shelly, and Goes just called me a little while ago," Rocky said. "Goes wants to get together tomorrow after school and not today, because Z has to go to dinner at her aunt's today and I have to go out to eat with my parents after church. So tomorrow we can all get together."

Four of the band members stood in a little circle outside Trenton High School on Monday afternoon. They talked together for a few minutes when Goes came running up to them. "Sorry I'm late. I had to sign up for Driver's Education in summer school," he said.

"You're lucky, you're sixteen already," Z said. "The rest of us will have to wait until next year to take Drivers Ed."

"Maybe I'll give you a ride someday, Z," Goes suggested.

"I'd rather ride a *donkey*," she answered.

---

donkey, see illustration page 16

donkey

"You love me, Z, and you know it."

Z gave him a look that would freeze the Atlantic Ocean. "You're a good drummer. Why don't we leave it at that."

Goes was about to say something, when Egghead spoke, "You two can talk about all that later. Right now we have to figure out what to do."

"I talked to my mother last night, and she said we should keep trying to call Sabrina Farley," Rocky said. The others thought about it for a minute and then agreed with him. They wanted to do more, but there was really nothing more for them to do.

"How about this," Shelly suggested. "I'll call today, and if I still get the machine, Goes can call tomorrow, and if he gets the machine, too, someone else can call the next day, and so on."

"Good idea," Egghead said, and they each took a day to call.

The went to their homes and met at Egghead's house to practice after they had eaten dinner. Shelly did not have any good news.

"I got the machine, and I left the same message – for her to call us," she told the others.

Her words were very disappointing. It took them an extra long time to set up their equipment and begin playing. It had been so easy the week before when they thought they had a chance to record a song, but now it felt like work.

"I've got a new song finished," Z said. "Do you want to try to play it?"

The others said they did.

"We've almost got enough songs for an album, but we don't have a single," Egghead said.

"So what!" Goes snapped. "We might as well keep playing."

"Playing for what?" Rocky asked. "Are we going to keep playing in a garage for the rest of our lives."

The five of them shot words across the room. Since the day when Sabrina Farley had not turned up, they had been arguing more and more.

"STOP! STOP! STOP!" Shelly screamed above the other voices. "We have to continue. If Sabrina Farley doesn't record a single for us, someone else will. But either way, we have to go on and keep playing."

The others looked at their shoes or down at their instruments. They knew Shelly was right. In a few minutes they were ready to play. Shelly played the melody of the new song on her *keyboard*. She gave a copy of the words to the others. Each one of them looked at the paper to figure out what part he or she would play in the song. Shelly played the music again and they sang along as best they could. After about ten tries, they could play the song through to the end, but it would take more time before it sounded good. Each time they played it, one or two of them would make a suggestion and they would try it a different way.

---

keyboard, musical instrument like a piano or organ

Their practices went the same way for the next three days. And they would start the same way — the one who tried to call Sabrina Farley would tell the others how there was no reply, but an answering machine. When they met on Friday evening, Egghead had some really bad news to tell them.

"Listen to this," Egghead said, as he led them to the telephone. He pushed some numbers, and then pushed the speaker button so the others could hear.

"Is that Sabrina Farley's number?" Rocky asked. Egghead nodded as they listened to the sound of the telephone ringing at the other end of the line.

After the third ring, they heard a woman's voice that sounded a bit mechanical: "The number you have dialed has been disconnected. Please check your telephone book to find the correct number."

"What does that mean?" Z asked.

"It could mean anything," Egghead answered.

"Maybe she got a new telephone number," Rocky suggested.

"No, I called information and there's no Sabrina Farley listed in the New York City area," Egghead answered.

"Maybe she moved her business to another city," Goes said.

"Or maybe she went out of business," Shelly said.

They thought about all the possibilities for a few seconds, and then Egghead said, "I just wish we would hear something from her. And I wish she would send back our micro-disc, so we could send it to another music company."

"Well, we can always record a new one," Shelly said. "I'd like to make some changes to that song we sent to her anyway."

They walked over to the garage, but they didn't play anything. They talked about their songs, their music and the future.

It's a Hit

During the next three weeks, they only practiced their music a few times. The school year was coming to a close and they had to study for their exams. It was on a Saturday morning in the beginning of June that Shelly got the shock of her life. She was cleaning up her room, listening to the radio as she worked. There were piles of books and papers and clothes scattered around the room. Her mother had told her that if she did not clean her room, she would come in with a big garbage bag and throw everything out.

While Shelly was trying to sort out the clean clothes from the dirty ones, a song came on the radio. She picked up a sweater and was trying to decide whether to wash it or not. Shelly could not make up her mind, and while she was thinking, she sang along with the radio.

It took around 20 or 30 seconds before she realized what she was listening to – and singing. It was a song that Z had written, the same one that they had sent to Sabrina Farley. The music was different, there was less guitar and more keyboards and what sounded like horns. But the *melody* and words were exactly the same.

Shelly sat down on the bed. Her lips formed the words of the song, but not a sound came from her mouth. She could hardly breathe, and her heart pounded like Goes' bass drum.

When the song had finished, the DJ's voice came through the radio. "That was 'Test Me' a brand new song, by a new band called Hook. You heard it first here

---

melody, the music in a song

20

21

on WJMJ-FM, and I'm sure you'll be hearing that number quite a bit from now on. It's already jumped up to number 38 on the Hot 100. I'm the Baron of Beat, the News of the Street, here on ..." Shelly raced from her room.

She turned the pages of the telephone book so the yellow pages flew by. "Radio stations, Radio stations," she said to herself as her finger went down the list of stations. With one finger by the number of WJMJ she worked the telephone with the other hand. "WJMJ", a woman's voice at the other end of the line said.

"Hello, I just heard a song called 'Test Me', and I would like to know more about the band, Hook."

The woman told Shelly that Hook was a band from the New York City area. There were three members, a singer named Sharon, a man named Nick Holmes who played guitars and bass, and a keyboard player named Bob Harper. Shelly asked who held the *copyright* to the song.

"Let me see," the woman said. After a few seconds, she answered: "SF Tunes."

Shelly thanked her and said good-bye. It took a few seconds before she realized what it probably meant. SF Tunes. SF – Sabrina Farley. Shelly almost fell over when she understood what it meant. She wanted to cry and she wanted to scream, but she was too angry to do either one. Sabrina Farley had stolen their song.

She grabbed the telephone again and dialed Z's number. Z wasn't home, so she tried Goes. He promised he

---

copyright: ©, the owner's rights to a work, such as a book or a song would meet her in 20 minutes, and said he would call Egghead.

Shelly sat talking to her mother and father when Goes arrived. "I got here as fast as I could," he told them. "Egghead said he can't get a ride into town, so he won't be coming."

"Rocky's out riding his bike, and Z wasn't home," Shelly told him. "But we have to do something."

"We have to drop your brother off at his soccer game," Shelly's father said. "And then we have to go grocery shopping. But when we get back, I'm going to call the other parents to find out if we can put a stop to this."

When her parents and brother had gone, Shelly told Goes what had happened since they had spoken on the phone. Her father had called the radio station and told the station *manager* the whole story. At first, the manager did not believe the story, but he listened anyway. The manager said that he could not help them, and ended their talk with: "Do you think that maybe the kids stole the song from Hook?" When Shelly's father heard this, his face turned red and he hung up the phone with a bang. Shelly's mother said that they would have to wait until Monday to do anything. Both she and her father promised to do everything they could.

When Shelly had finished telling Goes what had happened, tears flooded from her eyes. "We worked so hard..." She sucked in air. " ... and somebody steals our song."

Goes put his arms around her as she cried. "And they made a hit out of it."

---

manager: one who takes care of a band, or other star, and does the planning

Climbing the Charts

What happened during the next two weeks was even worse. 'Test Me' climbed to the top of the music charts. It was the Number One song in all of America, but it belonged to SF Tunes. It seemed that every time they turned on the radio, the song was being played.

All of their parents had tried to call people they thought could help, but nobody seemed to know what to do. They called different record companies, but they all said the same thing. If a person or company held the rights to music, it was theirs. Rocky's father called a lawyer who offered to take the case, but he also said that it would be difficult to win. They all felt as if there was no hope.

The only bright sign came on the last day of school. Rocky had to return some music books he had borrowed from the music teacher Mr. Baronski. He walked into the music room and said hello to the teacher who was doing some paperwork. Mr. Baronski was unusual. He was young, had very short hair and wore two earrings in his left ear. Sometimes the kids could see the tattoo he had on his left arm, if his shirt sleeves were rolled up. Many of the parents did not like him because he wore earrings and had a tattoo, but the unusual thing was – he hated pop music. Mr. Baronski only listened to Classical Music, and would not talk about anything else. But he was a good teacher.

"How's it going, Rocky?" Mr. Baronski asked as Rocky walked into the room.

"Hi Mr. B. I'm OK I guess," he answered.

"You don't look very OK. Is something wrong?" the teacher asked.

Rocky was tired of telling the story. It felt as if he had told it 1000 times, and maybe he had. But he told the story to Mr. Baronski anyway. The teacher listened.

"We've given up," Rocky finished. "There's nothing left for us to do. But the worst thing is, they play our song all the time on the radio."

"I wouldn't know. I don't listen to those kinds of radio stations," Mr. B said. "But I know that this type of thing happens all the time in the music business." He walked over to a low bookshelf and put his hand on top of Mozart's stone head. There were *busts* of Classical Music *composers* all around the room. He rubbed the head, thinking for a second and then continued. " I have a friend." He rubbed the head again. "Maybe he can help you."

Rocky looked at him as if he had lost his mind. He though Mr. B meant that Mozart could help.

"My friend Mike Rice from New York City works in the music business. He helps young musicians who are getting started in pop music. If you can call them musicians. You know, you should play classical guitar, and Shelly could be an opera singer, and Z can really write poetry, and ..." He stopped himself. "Come along with me. I'll give Mike a call."

Mr. B took an address book from his book bag, and Rocky followed him to the school office. He waited excitedly as Mr. B made the call. After a few seconds, Mr. B turned to Rocky. "It's his answering machine. What's

---

busts, small statues, usually just the head and shoulders of a person
composers, persons who write music

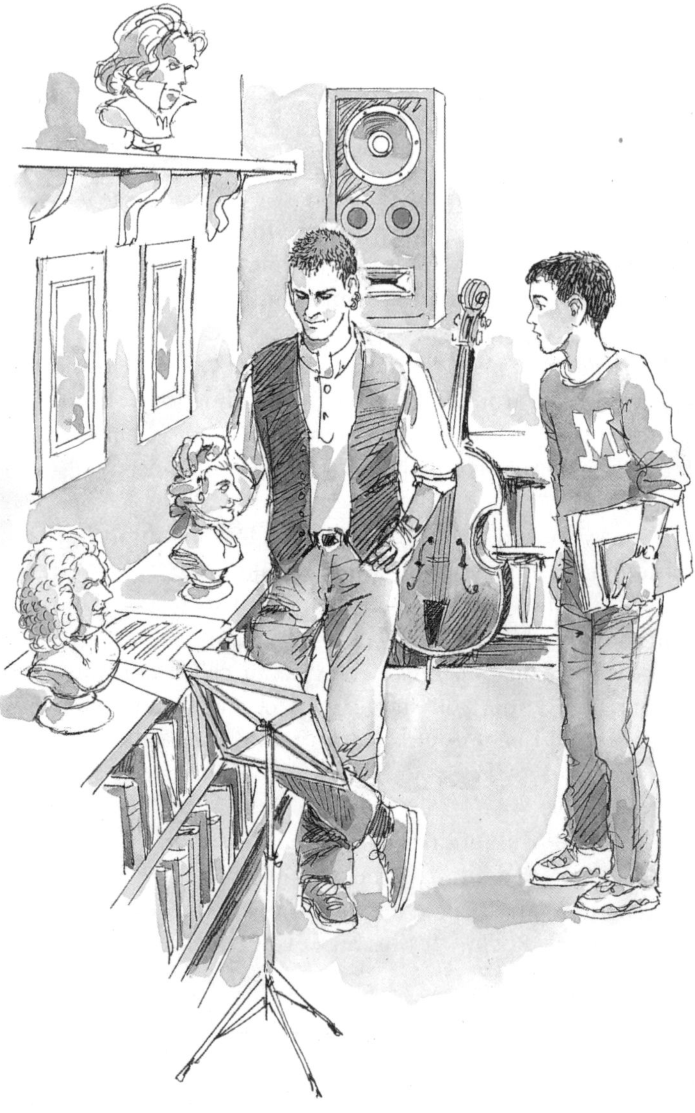

your phone number, I'll ask him to call you." Rocky wrote the number down on a piece of paper as Mr. B began to speak into the phone. "Hi Mike. This is Jim Baronski. Could you do me a favor, please, and call one of my students. He's a good kid and he and a few of his friends have a problem you may be able to help them with." He ended by giving Rocky's number.

"I hope Mike can help you," the teacher said.

"Thanks a million Mr. B. I hope so, too. I owe you a favor," Rocky said.

"You're right. You do owe me a favor and I know what it is. Come with me."

Rocky followed him back to the music room. Mr. B went to his CD rack, ran a finger along the row of CDs until he found what he was looking for. "This is some of the best classical guitar work ever done," he said, handing the CD to Rocky. "I want you to listen to this at least ten times this summer. You can give it back to me in September. And don't even try to tell me that you didn't like it. Good luck, and have fun this summer."

Rocky thanked him again and hurried out the door. When he got home he called the others to tell them the news.

Mike Rice

Every time the telephone rang, Rocky jumped up to answer it. And every time one of the others in his family would talk on the phone, he would stand there telling them to hurry up. At around seven o'clock, Mike Rice called.

Rocky could hardly get the word 'hello' out of his mouth when he heard it was Rice.

"Jim Baronski left a message for me to call you," Rice said.

Rocky explained who he was, and then began to tell the story of how Sabrina Farley had stolen their song. He was so excited, he could not find the right way to say it.

"So you think someone named Farley stole your song and is going to record it?" Rice asked.

"No, you don't understand. She did record it!"

"Have you seen it. Have you seen a CD album or a single?" Rice wanted to know.

"Yes, I mean no. I haven't seen a CD or anything, I've only head it on the radio."

"Do you mean that some local radio station up there plays this song that you say is yours?"

"They all play it. I'm talking about 'Test Me'. That's our song!" Rocky cried.

Rice did not speak for about 10 seconds. Finally, he said, "You're trying to tell me that 'Test Me', the Number One song in the country was written by a bunch of school kids?"

"Yes! We ..." Rocky did not get the chance to finish.

"I'm a businessman. I don't have time for school-kid jokes like this."

"But we did!"

"Good-bye!" Rice said, and the telephone clicked in Rocky's ear. He stood there looking at the phone for several seconds. Rocky felt that all hope was now gone. He walked up to his room and flopped down onto the bed. The others should hear about what Rice had to say, but Rocky did not feel like calling anyone.

Around half an hour later, his father called up the stairs to him. Somebody wanted to talk to him on the telephone. Rocky almost said he would call the person back, but he went downstairs anyway. When he heard Mike Rice's voice on the other end, his heart pounded.

"Hi, this is Mike Rice again. I guess I should say I'm sorry for hanging up the phone earlier. Your story sounded like something from a bad TV show – in fact it still does. But I called Jim Baronski, and he told me that you and your friends are all good kids. He didn't think you were making all this up," Rice said. "Jim doesn't know anything about pop music, but he does know about people. So, tell me your story once again."

Rocky was glad to repeat the story.

Rice had one question. "Do you have the song on tape? Something that can prove that it was written by you and your friends, and prove when it was written?"

Rocky's heart sank into his shoes. "I don't know. I don't think so. Egghead, I mean my friend Roger, only recorded it once on micro-disc," he said.

"Look, Rocky, I have to say this as directly as I can," Rice said. "If you have a tape of the song, you might – and I mean might – have a little chance of winning a case. If you have a tape, a *musicologist* could listen to it

---

musicologist, a person who is a music expert

and decide whether Hook used your music."

"But the song is exactly the same. It's our song. The other band didn't change the words or the music, only the instruments are different," Rocky cried.

"Listen to me. You sent someone a song on a microdisc. You didn't get the song, neither the music nor the lyrics, registered anywhere. If you register music, you own it. If you don't, the person who does register it owns it. SF Tunes owns your song," Rice said. "You might just as well have sent this Sabrina Farley a million dollars cash. She received it and can do what she wants with it. In fact, the way that record is selling, you probably did send her a million dollars."

The words cut into Rocky like a knife. "Couldn't we go to a newspaper and tell our story?" he asked.

"You could do that, but you would still have to prove that the song is yours. If a newspaper wrote the story, it would be saying that SF Tunes stole something. If you can't prove that they did, you could get into a lot of trouble and SF Tunes would still own the song," Rice said.

"I'll be happy to help you, but you have to help me. I'll try to find out who this Sabrina Farley is," Rice explained. "And you kids have to come up with a tape of that song, and anything else that can help to prove it's yours. I don't suppose you have sheet music for the song."

"No, none of us can write music that well," Rocky said.

"I didn't think so," Rice answered. "It would have helped, but the main thing is a tape.."

"I'll call my friends and hear if they have anything on tape," Rocky said.

"Good. I'll do what I can from this end," Rice said. "But listen to me. Even if you do find a tape, you may not win. I've seen cases like this before, and they can go either way. So, don't get your hopes up."

"Don't worry. We haven't had any hope for a long time," Rocky said.

"We'll fight them if we can. I'll give you a call in a few days and let you know if I've got any information for you," Rice said.

"Thank you," Rocky answered. "But tell me something. Why are you doing this for us? Are you doing it because Mr. Baronski asked you to?"

Rice chuckled for a second. "I told you before, I'm a businessman. If you kids really made that song, I'm going to be the one who helps you get a record contract. And that's how I earn my money. I'll talk to you soon."

Rocky waited for a few minutes before calling Egghead. He crossed his fingers and hoped that Egghead had another copy of the song. In the other room, his younger sister Julie was listening to the radio. She turned up the sound when she heard her favorite song. Rocky heard a song that made his stomach turn round and round.

"TURN IT DOWN!" he shouted, as he started to call Egghead.

Egghead's search

Egghead answered the telephone himself. Rocky explained what Mike Rice had said to him, that they needed to have their song on tape or micro-disc to prove that it was theirs..

"Oh boy," Egghead said.

"What do you mean, 'Oh boy?'"

"I mean I hope I have that song on a disc," Egghead said. "I'll take a look and call you back later. Can you call the others and tell them what Mike Rice said to you?"

Rocky told him that he would, and they hung up.

Egghead ran to his room. He pulled out all the micro-discs he had – seven in all – and began feeding them into the player. One by one, he listened to all the recordings he had made of the band. Some of them had their own songs, and others had popular songs by other bands. There were even some recordings where he could hear the band members arguing about how to play a song.

It took a long time to go through the first disc. Egghead remembered recording some of the things as he heard them. He had got the disc player/recorder for his last birthday, and the first two discs he had made sounded bad, because he was just learning how to use the machine. The second disc had music he had written himself, but no recordings of the band. Egghead fed another into the machine and pushed the 'PLAY' button. He heard the music that the band had written themselves. A song would start, play for a few seconds and then someone would make a mistake and the music stopped. Voices talking about what to do, or how to do it. More music. More voices.

And then Egghead found it. He heard the first part of 'Test Me.' It played for maybe half a minute, then Z began to talk: "No, that's not right. Try an A-minor Rocky, and Goes pick up on the drums." Rocky said something, and Egghead could hear that he was far away from the microphone. "One, two ... one, two, three, four," Z said, and the music began again.

Egghead's heart pounded. This was it. The band went through the whole song, and there could be no mistake in anybody's ears that they were playing 'Test Me.'

He raced to the telephone. As he began to call Rocky, Egghead's mother said, "It's almost eleven o' clock. Who do you think you're calling."

"Rocky. He's expecting me to call him."

Rocky let out a shout of pure joy when Egghead told him that he had found the song. "I'll listen to the other two discs to hear if the song's on them," Egghead said. "I'm sure it's there, both the whole song and parts of it."

When he had said good-bye to Rocky, Egghead told his mother and father about what had happened. They both said that it sounded good, but told him that he would have to wait until the next day to make any more phone calls.

The next day, the band met at Rocky's house. Egghead took two discs with him, and his player. They listened to the song. When it ended, they jumped up and down hugging each other and 'slapping fives.'

"We did it!" Goes cried. He played a drum roll in the air.

"Now we have to call Mike Rice and tell him the news," Shelly said.

They stood around Rocky as he called Mike Rice's number. It took a long time for Rice to answer.

"Hello, Mr. Rice. This is Rocky Stone, I mean Bob Stone. We talked last night."

The others watched with great smiles on their faces as he spoke. Rocky told Mike Rice about the discs, and how they had the whole song a couple of times and parts of the song on the two discs. He could hardly talk, he was so excited. Shelly's head was pressed against Rocky's head as she listened to the tiny voice in the telephone.

Z was the first to see the change on Rocky's face.

"But .." Rocky whispered. "But we ... "

Mike Rice had bad news. "Listen Rocky. The music on the discs isn't enough. As I said last night, you need to prove when you recorded the song, too. Just because you have a song on a disc, doesn't mean that you did it first. Some could say that you recorded the song yesterday, and not months ago."

"But we did!" Rocky *insisted*.

"I believe you. I'm on your side. But think about it – if you went into a *court* of law, you would never win. Right now there are probably hundreds of bands, all across America, who are playing that song. Any one of them could record it and say that it's theirs. You need to prove WHEN you recorded it."

Z, Egghead and Goes couldn't hear what Rice was saying, but they could see on Rocky's and Shelly's faces that something was wrong. Shelly sat down and started to cry. Goes put a hand on her shoulder.

"But ..." was all that Rocky could say. Tears filled his eyes.

---

insist, to say strongly one is right
court, place where questions of law are decided

"And by the way, I've found out who this Sabrina Farley is," Rice said. "Her real name is Samantha Connor. She has a partner named Richard Sam Capo. They've done this kind of thing before. They had a company called Sam and Sam that would either steal songs or buy them for next to nothing – which was the same as stealing – and make money on them. Or they would sign a band, make the band work and they would keep the money. I found this out from a friend of mine in the music business. The sad thing is, it was all legal. Kids like yourselves want to be pop stars and will do almost anything to get there. They write their names on a *contract* that they haven't read, or send in tapes or discs as you did. And there's nothing that can be done.

"But this is the first time they have ever had a hit. And I'm sorry that it happened to you."

Rocky could not talk.

"I'm sorry to say so, but you should forget 'Test Me.' You can't win. Believe me. You can't possibly win unless you can prove when you made the song. But if you have more music, I would be happy to help. Just make sure you have copies, dated copies, next time," Rice said.

"Thank you," Rocky said, and put down the phone.

The band members looked at each other. There was nothing to do, and nothing to say.

---

contract, a paper that tells the rules of business between two sides

Mr. Willis

Egghead got a ride home with his mother, who worked at the video store in town. She asked him questions, and he gave short answers.

"I'm so sorry, Roger. I wish there was something I or you father could do, but it sounds as if Mike Rice knows what he's talking about," she said. "Oh, why do people have to be so mean. How could they steal from children."

Egghead did not like to hear the word children, but right now he felt like a helpless child.

When they got home, Egghead told his parents he was going over to the garage to listen to some music. He put on an old Nirvana CD and turned it up loud. There was an old air mattress on a shelf, so Egghead took it down and filled it with air. Then he placed it on the floor and lay on top of it.

Egghead felt as if he had a big stone inside him. He closed his eyes and tried to listen to the loud music. It helped a little, but not much. All he could think about was how helpless he felt. Sabrina Farley, or whatever her name was, had stolen their song and there was nothing to be done about it. They could have become pop stars. But, no, they had made a foolish mistake by sending the disc to her. How could they know that this would happen?

Egghead wanted to cry, he wanted to scream, he wanted to throw his keyboard through the window. He wanted their song back.

After a few minutes, he got up and turned up the music. Maybe if it was loud enough, it would take away the bad feelings inside him. Egghead lay back down on the mattress. He was sure that in a little while, his mother, or father, or sister would come over to the garage and tell him to turn it down, but he didn't care. Right now all he wanted to do was not think about the whole situation.

Sure enough, in a few seconds his little sister Julie opened the door. "Mom says you have to turn down the music," his sister shouted. She stood there with a finger in each ear.

"All right, but get out of here. I want to be alone," he answered.

"It's my garage, too!" Julie said, stuck out her tongue and slammed the door.

As he got up from the mattress, Egghead walked over to the stereo. As he turned the *volume* knob, a thought hit him like a bowling ball to the head. "Loud music!" he said out loud, and ran for the door.

Egghead burst through the door. He tripped over his sister's bicycle which stood outside the garage and fell flat on his face. It did not stop him. His feet kept moving and he ran across the grass and onto the road.

"Oh, please, please, please, please," his sister heard him say as he dashed past her. Julie watched as Egghead ran down the road.

It felt as if his legs could not move fast enough. He tried to run faster, but he was already moving at top speed. Egghead heard the sound of a lawn mower ahead of him. In a few seconds, he saw Mr. Willis pushing the mower. Egghead ran to where Mr. Willis was. When he got close, he tried to stop on the newly-cut

---

volume, loudness

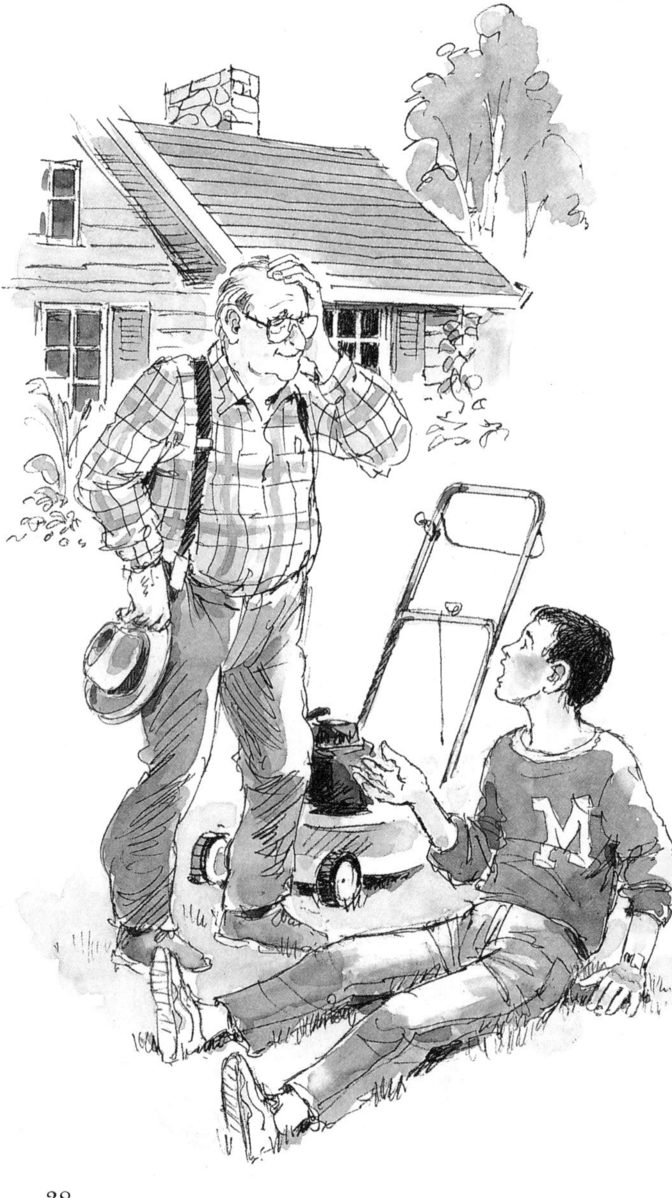
M

grass, but his legs went out from under him. He landed right on his behind.

"Mr. Willis! Mr. Willis!" he cried to the old man.

Mr. Willis turned off the motor. He took off his cap and ran a hand through the few hairs that were still on his head. "Well, well. If it isn't Trenton's own Elvis Presley," the old man said.

Egghead jumped to his feet. "Mr. Willis, I'm sorry we play loud music, but this is important," he said. His could hardly talk after running all the way.

"Oh, don't worry. I was young once, too. Why, Mrs. Willis and I used to play Benny Goodman pretty loud ourselves back in the old days," he began. "But now my wife likes to get to bed early, and sometimes she can't sleep when she hears you kids playing that music. And then she gets angry with me."

Egghead did not have the time to hear one of Mr. Willis' long stories. The man could talk for days if given the chance. "Mr. Willis, please listen to me!" he said. "It's important."

Mr. Willis could see that Egghead had something important to say. "Go ahead," he replied.

"Do you remember that tape you have of us playing?"

"Sure. But it wasn't me who did it. It was my wife. She..."

Egghead didn't give him a chance to finish. "I need to hear that tape!"

As they walked toward the house, Egghead told him as much of the story as he could. Mr. Willis listened and shook his head. "That would have never happened in the old days."

When they got into the house, Mrs. Willis said hello and asked them if they wanted a glass of lemonade. Egghead said no, but Mr. Willis said, "I'd love one, honey."

He went to find the tape as Mrs. Willis poured two glasses of lemonade. She handed one to Egghead and he gulped it down fast.

Mr. Willis walked back into the kitchen with a tape in his hand. "Here it is."

"May I borrow it?" Egghead asked, reaching for the tape.

"Why sure," Mr. Willis answered, and handed it to him.

"Thanks, Mr. Willis. Thanks a million." Egghead headed to the door. "And thanks for the lemonade, Mrs. Willis. I'll return this later."

Egghead ran home, and into the garage. His hands shook as he put the tape into the player. The first thing he heard was a radio program the Willis' had taped. Egghead pushed the 'Fast Forward' button. More radio, and then some music, but it was not what he was looking for. Egghead looked at the tape in the machine. There was only a thin roll of tape left. He played it to the end, but the recording he was looking for was not there.

Quickly, he pushed 'Eject' and turned the tape around. The first thing he heard sounded as if it had been recorded in outer space. He could hear the wind, and then a bird. There was a noise in the background that sounded like something WHOOSHING past. "Cars on the highway," Egghead thought. Drops of sweat popped out of his forehead. Was this it?

And then it came. First, Rocky's guitar, followed by the booming sound of Z's bass and Goes on drums. In a second, he could hear Z's voice, and the keyboards. The sound came from far away. It would be clear for a few seconds, and then it would fade away. But one thing was certain – Egghead could hear the melody of 'Test Me.' He turned off the tape player and ran to the house.

Crossed Fingers

"Give me Mike Rice's phone number," Egghead shouted into the telephone.

Rocky knew it was Egghead on the other end, but did not know what he meant. He started to say something, but Egghead repeated what he had said.

"Why?" Rocky wanted to know.

Egghead told him about the tape. "Do you think it will be enough?" Rocky asked.

"I don't know. But I'm keeping my fingers crossed."

Rocky gave him Mike Rice's number, and he made the call. Mike Rice listened to what Egghead had to say. When he had finished, Egghead waited. It took a few seconds before Rice began to speak.

"That sounds good, very good in fact," Rice told him. "Can you get the man, what was his name?"

"Mr. Willis."

"Can you get him to sign a *statement* saying when he taped the music?" Rice asked.

"I'm sure he will."

"Good." Rice said nothing for several seconds. "I think we have a chance."

Egghead's heart almost jumped out of his chest when he heard this. "Now listen," Rice continued. "First, make a copy of the tape. Make two, in fact. Then get this Mr. Willis to write a statement saying when he made the tape. This statement will have to be signed by a *public* official, to show that it is real. Make a couple of copies

---

statement, to say, or write something as truth
public, working for the government

of the statement, too. Send them to me, and I will send you a paper that will give me the right to try to win this case for you. A friend of mine is a musicologist. If he can say that the music on the tape is the same as the song that Hook made, then we have a chance."

"I'll do all that right away. Right now," Egghead answered.

"Good. But listen, this could take me a couple of weeks, or a couple of months," Rice explained. "And we could still lose. So, don't get your hopes up too high. I'll do my best."

"I'll get going right now," Egghead said.

"Wait just a minute," Rice said. "No matter what happens, I think you kids should keep playing your music. Work hard. Practice every day. And when you get some songs, record them for me. Just remember to register the songs. Don't make the same mistake twice."

"Don't worry. We won't," Egghead promised. "I'll send you the tape and statement as soon as I can."

Egghead started to go out the door to go back to the Willis', but then he remembered something. He went to the telephone again and called Mike Rice.

"What's your address? I forgot to ask you."

When he had finished talking to Rice, he went back to speak with Mr. Willis. By the time he had got the statement from Mr. Willis, it was too late to get an official to sign it. It would have to wait until Monday.

Egghead called the other band members and told them what had happened. He asked them to come to his house on the following day.

When they all were there, inside the garage, Egghead played the tape for them.

"It sounds terrible," Z said when she heard it.

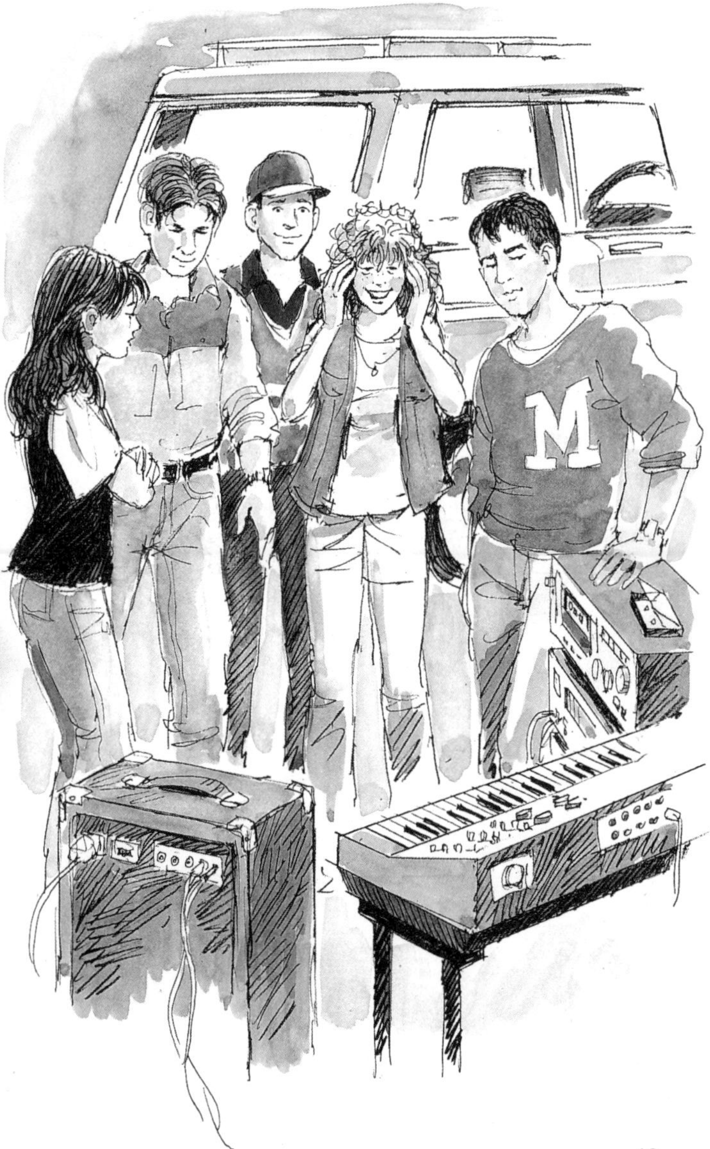
M

"I think it sounds beautiful," Goes said.

"Me too," Shelly added. "If only it will help us to win our song back."

They talked about whether they should play some music, but decided it was too nice of a day to be inside. Rocky suggested that they go to the river to swim, so they did.

On Monday, Egghead's mother drove Mr. Willis and her son to the Trenton Town Hall, where they got an official to sign Mr. Willis' statement. The woman in the office took two copies of the statement. From there they went to the post office and sent the statement and tape to Mike Rice. Egghead went from the post office over to Shelly's house, and his mother drove home with Mr. Willis.

"Now all we have to do is wait," Shelly said.

"Yeah, that's all," Egghead said. He looked at the second hand on his watch moving very slowly.

Win Some, Lose Some

A week went by. Then two. Several times they talked about whether they should call Mike Rice, but decided it was best to wait. But waiting was not easy.

To make the time go faster, they practiced their music. They would meet at Egghead's house each morning and play until around noon. After a quick lunch, they would go down and swim in the river under the hot sun.

Every time the telephone rang in one of their homes, they would jump up in hopes that it was Mike Rice. They had send him all their telephone numbers, just in case one of them was not home when Rice called.

Mike Rice called Rocky on a Wednesday night. "My friend, the musicologist, has listened to your tape," he said. "And he has written a statement saying that he believes the music is yours."

Rocky was so filled with joy he could have jumped to the moon.

"That was a couple of weeks ago," Rice continued. "I've brought the case into a court here in New York, and a decision is expected to be made tomorrow at ten. I'll call you as soon as I hear something."

"OK, I'll tell the others," Rocky said, and was about to hang up the phone, but Rice stopped him.

"Wait a minute," Rice said. "I told you before that I earn my living in the music business. And I want to try to do something with you kids. Now, I've tried to help you, so I want you to promise me that when you have some music finished and recorded, I'll be your man."

"We'll send you our promise in writing," Rocky said.

"I don't think I need a piece of paper," Rice said, and he was right.

The next day, the five of them met at Rocky's house. They talked and laughed for a while, but at five minutes to ten they became silent. All they could do was watch the telephone, waiting and hoping it would ring.

At 10:22 it rang.

"Well, I've got good news and I've got bad news," Mike Rice said to Rocky.

"Wait just a second, I'm going to switch on the telephone speaker so the others can hear you," Rocky said, and pushed a button.

"The good news is you won. 'Test Me' is your song." He had to wait before speaking. The five band members shouted and laughed with happiness when they heard his words. After a few seconds Rice continued: "The bad news is you won the case, but you really didn't win anything."

The five of them looked at each other with questions on their faces.

"The song is yours. There can be no question about that," Rice explained. "But it's already been a hit. It came out more than a month ago, and now it's off most of the music charts, and radio stations will not be allowed to play it any more. The record is illegal, so we have to tell the stations not to play it, and they won't. But this all means that it's history. It's an old song. Even if you recorded it again, with your names on it, it wouldn't be played because it is an old song."

"Couldn't we record it anyway and stations could play it as an *oldie*?" Z asked him.

"It wouldn't be worth it. Stations would only play it once in a while, if at all. Forget about that," Rice said.

---

oldie, an old song

"But this story gets worse."

The five of them wondered how much worse it could get.

"Sabrina Farley or Samantha Connor or whatever her name is and her partner Sam Culver, and SF Tunes or whatever company name they use, have all disappeared. The names were probably false. The companies they used didn't have offices, just post box addresses. That's why they only used mobile phones. They made the record themselves and they made the money. There could be some payments from record sales, but it would cost you so much to try and get this money, it wouldn't be worth it."

"Do you mean we won't get anything?" Goes asked.

"I don't think so," Rice said. "They get to keep the money, unless the police find them, and they will probably never find them."

Rocky held the phone in his hand. He didn't know what to say and neither did his friends. They had won when there was nothing to win.

"Look. A song that was Number One in America is yours. I know it's not a lot, but think about it. In a little while, people will know that five kids from Trenton, New York made a song that was a hit," Rice said. "And these five kids will be making more music. Right?"

It took a few seconds before they could answer. He was right, but it didn't help the empty feeling they all had.

"You kids get to work," Rice said. "Make me some music, and I'll see to it that you make records. Call me when you have something."

"Thanks Mr. Rice," Rocky said, and the others said the same.

It took a long time before any of them could say a

word. They sat or stood looking out into space.

"That was our best song," Shelly finally said.

"Yeah, it was," Goes agreed.

"How can we ever make another one as good as that. The reason we sent Sabrina Farley 'Test Me' was because it was the best," Z said.

"Well, we'll just have to make another one that's as good or better," Rocky said. "We've got other songs. We can work on them and we'll come up with something."

"You're right," Z said. "It would be silly to stop now. We've worked so hard."

Egghead was about to say something when the telephone rang. Rocky answered it. He listened for a few seconds and then held his hand over the mouthpiece. "It's Rolling Stone magazine. Mike Rice told them our story, and now they want to do an article about us, or about how our song was stolen."

"We'll be famous," Goes said. "The pop group that hit number one, but never made a record."

"It's a start," Z said. "We might as well tell them the story."

"Maybe some other kids will read it and it will help them," Shelly added.

"OK, let's talk to them," Egghead said. "It could be the start of our career."

Questions

Who are the five members of the band? What instruments do they play?

Describe the town, area, where they live?

Do you know anybody who has a band like this one?

Is modern music changing?

Do you think they did a silly thing by sending Sabrina Farley their tape?

Do you play an instrument? Which one?

Have you ever tried to record a song?

What would be a good name for a band?

Who is your favorite pop artist, and why?

Do you read magazines or newspapers about pop stars?

Do you watch MTV, or a channel like it? Why?

Are there any pop artists whom both you and your parents/teachers like?

Do you listen to the radio? How often? What do you listen to?

Has anybody ever stolen anything from you?

Have you ever heard or read about a story like this one – where music has been stolen?

Do pop artists make too much money?

How do the youngsters' parents try to help?

What does Mike Rice do for them?

What do you think will happen to the five of them in the future? Will they stay together? Will they become pop stars?

Notes: